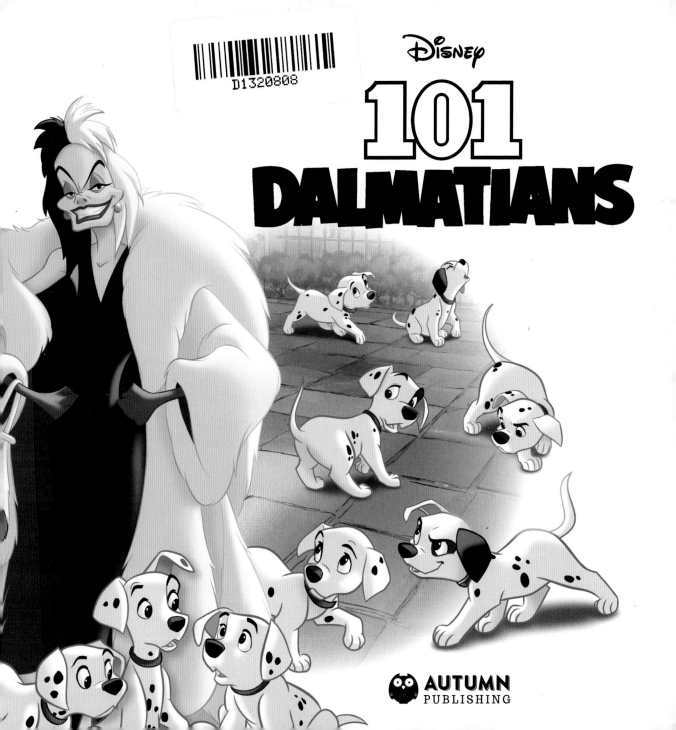

Disney

101 DALMATIANS

AUTUMN PUBLISHING

Roger was a musician. He lived in a flat with Pongo, his pet Dalmatian.

One day, while walking Pongo, Roger met a woman called Anita. She owned a lady Dalmatian called Perdita.

Roger and Anita fell in love, and decided to get married.

Soon, Perdita was expecting her first litter of puppies. Life seemed perfect until, one day, an old friend of Anita's, Cruella De Vil, came to visit. Perdita and Pongo were frightened of her.

Cruella stormed inside looking for the puppies. "Where are the little brutes?" she demanded.

"It'll be at least three weeks," replied Anita. "No rushing these things, you know."

Anita offered Cruella a cup of tea, but Cruella couldn't stay. "Let me know when the puppies arrive," said Cruella. "Cheerio, darling!"

With that, Cruella slammed the door and was gone.

Three weeks later, during a dark and stormy October night, Pongo and Perdita became the proud parents of fifteen perfect puppies. Roger, Anita and Nanny, the housekeeper, were delighted.

That same night, as lightning flashed and thunder rumbled, Cruella returned. "Fifteen puppies!" she cried, excitedly. "How marvellous. I'll take them all!"

"We're not selling the puppies," said Roger, who wasn't going to put up with Cruella's demands any more. "Not a single one."

"Just wait," cried Cruella, angrily. "You'll be sorry, you fools. You idiots!"

A few weeks later, when the puppies were older and had their spots, Cruella's henchmen, Horace and Jasper Badun, lay in wait to dognap the puppies. They sat in their van and waited for Roger and Anita to take Perdita and Pongo for their evening walk.

Once the coast was clear, the Baduns forced their way into the house. When Nanny tried to stop them, the Baduns locked her in Roger's music room.

By the time Nanny managed to escape, the Baduns were gone – and so were the puppies!

The police immediately launched an investigation, but as the days went by, the puppies were still not found.

After realising the humans weren't getting anywhere, Pongo said to Perdita, "I'm afraid it's all up to us."

Pongo decided to try the Twilight Bark. This was the quickest way for dogs to send and receive news across the country.

That evening, when the two Dalmatians were taken for their walk, Pongo barked the alert from the top of Primrose Hill.

After a moment, an answering bark was heard. "It's the Great Dane at Hampstead!" Pongo said to Perdita, and he barked out his message.

Danny the Great Dane was very surprised by the message. "Fifteen Dalmatian puppies stolen!" he told a terrier friend. "The humans have tried everything. Now it's up to us dogs. The Twilight Bark!"

Danny's big deep voice began to send the news all over London...

Within the hour, word had spread north, south, east and west – all over England.

Before too long, the Twilight Bark reached an old sheepdog called Colonel, who lived on a farm.

Colonel's friends – a horse named Captain and a cat named Sergeant Tibbs – listened too. They were all very surprised to hear that fifteen puppies had been stolen!

"I just remembered," Tibbs said to Captain and Colonel. "Two nights past, I heard puppy barking over at Hell Hall."

"You mean the old De Vil place? No one's lived there for years," said Colonel. "Strange, indeed. Well, I suppose we better investigate."

So Colonel and Tibbs went quietly up to the manor house. Being small enough, Tibbs was able to sneak inside. He saw Horace and Jasper Badun were eating supper and relaxing in front of the television.

All round the room there were puppies. Not fifteen – nor even fifty – but ninety-nine of them!

Colonel quickly returned to Captain's stable and loudly barked the good news. Within no time at all, the Twilight Bark sent the message all the way back to London that the puppies had been found.

It finally reached the ears of Perdita and Pongo. They set off across the snowy countryside as fast as they could to rescue their puppies.

Meanwhile, Tibbs was keeping watch on the house. When he saw Cruella drive up to Hell Hall, he went up to the manor to hear what was happening.

Cruella was ordering the Baduns to kill the puppies! "It's got to be done tonight!" she cried. "I'll be back first thing in the morning." With that warning hanging in the air, she turned and was gone.

Tibbs was horrified Cruella wanted to kill the puppies! There wasn't a moment to lose.

As soon as the Baduns began watching television again, Tibbs crept through a hole in the wall and whispered to the nearest puppies, "You better get out of here, if you want to save your skins."

When all the puppies had been alerted, Tibbs led them to a hiding place in the manor.

As soon as the Baduns discovered that the puppies had gone, they searched all over the house and eventually found them cowering under the stairs. Tibbs was in front, ready to protect them from the Baduns.

Meanwhile, Colonel had met up with Perdita and Pongo and led them to the manor house. They arrived just in the nick of time and quickly bounded into action.

Perdita attacked Horace, while Pongo tore at Jasper's trousers.

Under cover of the fight, Tibbs led the puppies out of the house to the safety of Captain's stable.

Leaving the Baduns in a heap on the floor,
Perdita and Pongo dashed after the puppies.

"Everybody here?" asked Pongo. "All fifteen?"

"Twice that many, Dad," replied one of the
puppies. "Now there's ninety-nine of us."

"What on earth would she want with so
many?" asked Perdita, wondering what Cruella
was planning.

"She's going to make coats out of us," said
another puppy, sadly.

Pongo and Perdita were shocked and decided
to take all the puppies back to London with
them so they'd be safe.

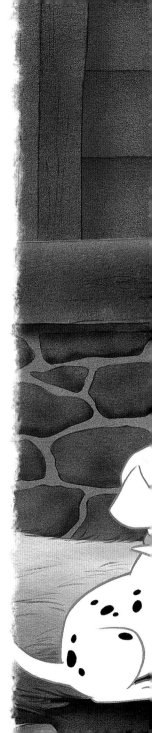

Perdita, Pongo and the puppies set off back to
London, leaving a trail of paw prints in the snow.
Cruella, who had returned for the puppies' coats,
quickly spotted the paw prints, and the chase began!

Eventually, after trudging across the cold countryside, Perdita and Pongo led the tired puppies to the shelter of a blacksmith's shop. Cruella and the Baduns were still on their trail, determined to catch them.

Suddenly, Pongo had an idea. He made the puppies roll in some soot until they all looked like black Labradors.

Under the cover of their disguise, the puppies climbed into a van that was going to London. But falling snowflakes began to wash away the soot.

Cruella saw white patches appearing on the puppies' coats and realised that she had been tricked. "After them!" she shouted to the Baduns.

Pongo just had time to leap onto the bumper as the van sped off – with Cruella and the Baduns right behind.

Cruella was determined to force the van off the road. But her car skidded out of control and hurtled down a steep hill into a snowdrift.

Then the Baduns' van crashed into the back of Cruella's car – and they all ended up in a large pile of wreckage!

Back in London and home at last, Roger, Anita and Nanny hugged their fifteen tired puppies.

"And look, there's a whole lot more," said Nanny.

Roger, Anita and Nanny counted up all the dogs in their house.

"A hundred and one!" declared Anita. "What will we do with them?"

"We'll keep them!" cried Roger, happily.

"In this little house?" asked Anita.

"We'll buy a big place in the country," replied Roger.

"It'll be a sensation," said Nanny.

And that's exactly what it was!